BETWEEN SHADOWS

BETWEEN SHADOWS

Tales and poems in quarantine

María del Pilar Martínez Nandín

Copyright © 2021 María del Pilar Martínez Nandín.

First edition, 2021
Author's email: mar_nandin@hotmail.com
Translation: Adriana Castro

All rights reserved. No part of this book may be reproduced in any form or by any electronic or mechanical means, including information storage and retrieval systems, without permission in writing from the publisher, except by reviewers, who may quote brief passages in a review.

ISBN: 978-1-63821-620-9 (Paperback Edition)
ISBN: 978-1-63821-621-6 (Hardcover Edition)
ISBN: 978-1-63821-619-3 (E-book Edition)

Some characters and events in this book are fictitious. Any similarity to real persons, living or dead, is coincidental and not intended by the author.

Book Ordering Information

Phone Number: 315 288-7939 ext. 1000 or 347-901-4920
Email: info@globalsummithouse.com
Global Summit House
www.globalsummithouse.com

Printed in the United States of America

In the shadows I look for myself,
in the shadows I hide,
in the shadows I find myself.

The girl I was
says GOODBYE to the past ...

INSTANTS

(July 18th)

In my yard
a dove and a cat live together in the same space.

SHE ... without being scared,
HE ... without attacking.

Her world: that tree. A happy world!

(July 10th)

For moments I relive, when I see them.

The past is present and the present is read
not in presences ... in PHOTOS.

(July 6th)

July's moon, moon of forever
It lights up!
darkness of the night.
Prevents the visit of thieves and for moments
steals my sleep

Eternal lantern! Keep shining ...

(July 4th)

They say that women are a dove for the nest.
I like it!

This little pigeon knows instinctively that you have to strengthen the branches and take care of its chicks.
How many women have forgotten?

(June 27th)

Butterflies like to visit
the tiny flowers of the rosemary.

This 2020 Palm Sunday was canceled. Inside the house there is not the blessed sprig of palm, rosemary and chamomile.

God bless my yard with the sacred plant.
It cheers everyone who passes.

Thank my Lord!

(June 26th)

Jasmine blooms in my window
What a joy when I open the door and they give
me their delicious aroma!

If beauty is in your house, I assure you,
You are in good company!

(June 21st)

This little bird fell out of the nest, its legs were not holding it ...
I thought
I must put it in place.
I was about to do it when he had already taken
momentum, it reached the edge of the planter and WASH!
It spread its wings ...
it climbed and flew towards the nearest branch ...

What a short childhood birds have!

(June 12th)

With a cracked voice, with a slow pace, with a calm soul,
I walk through the desert.

Silence helps ...
brings me closer to the ETERNAL!

(April)

This beautiful cardinal crossed like red lightning
(looking for something to eat
or quench its thirst); I barely saw it, through the
window, I wanted to capture it ...
but my photo does not reflect clearly
its beauty.

Between Tale And...

Between Tale and Reality

(May 11th)

Quarantine Effects

I read some verses by Alberto Cortez that say: "It would be without an order the snack / to eat each other ONE".

In crises I have found that what comes to the surface the better or worse of the human being.

This contingency teaches me that: "A troubled river, fishermen win", a saying that does not lose validity.

I am certain that when vandalism invades, the first thing affected is PRIVATE PROPERTY. If we let these acts proliferate, shielded by the fact that the properties are alone, we will end up giving wings to the thieves even though the houses are occupied ... It reminds me of the MEXICAN REVOLUTION ... Hidden in the ball, they destroyed and looted.

I hope in GOD that this situation does not last and that the Public Ministries, Property Registry, Offices, Notaries' offices and others will function normally again.

We are defending ourselves against COVID, that the GOVERNMENT works as it should and defends a fundamental principle: PRIVATE PROPERTY.

Between Tale and Legend

(May 10th)

Death has permission ...

Today the funeral parks are alone. We were unable to bring flowers to mothers, or visit other loved ones.

The only one that walks around and the whole world is the DEATH ... she has permission.

They say that he came to a village to take the oldest of them. Among them was Panchita, but when he knocked on her door, no one answered. A neighbor shouted: "Pancha went to see the sick at the nursing home." Ms. Death ran and asked for "Panchita!", But she had already gone to bring flowers to the Virgin ... She entered the church and did not find her. The sacristan told him: "Doña Francisca is taking food to the men in the plots." The undesirable continued looking for her chosen one, she did not find her ... The peasants reported: "Pancha went to feed the animals."

Death, who is so fair, thought: "This old lady is a hard worker, I will let her continue in her MISSION." Singing he walked away (Life is worth nothing ... life is worth nothing), and in order not to leave empty-handed, he took a skinny cow ...

Between Tale and Gossip

(May 9th)

The snow ball

When I worked at the IMSS, as a consulting assistant, I saw the waiting room FULL.

It amused me to listen to the people's conversation ... "Hey, this flu that doesn't go away every time gets uglier, he shot my old man down"; "My girl doesn't pay attention, she bathes early and she already had a choking cough…", "It's ANDANCIA", they concluded ...

Yes! The disease was rampant, but no one was afraid and they passed a few prescriptions before consulting with their doctor ... When the waiting room was half empty the doctors expressed: "There is a HEALTH EPIDEMIC."

Yesterday I visited a hospital for a suture that was done in an isolated office, with all the security measures. The empty parking lot, the empty waiting room, the pharmacy too ... I reminded my doctors: "There is a health EPIDEMIC ...".

I wondered ... then COVID DOES NOT WALK?

It has paralyzed everything and at least, here, in my city it does not work ... The snowball grows ... This enemy is rare, it is not seen and it causes FEAR ... I am looking forward to a day without COVID.

BETWEEN TALE AND GOSSIP

(May 2th)

Do they sell us air?

I have observed, for some time, that everything is SELLING us. My grandparents used to say: "A glass of water is not denied to anyone." Today they sell it to you. (Water, Earth, Fire, Air) the 4 vital elements to exist are being handled by unscrupulous hands, without CONSCIOUSNESS.

I thought that air was not being sold because they had not found a way to do it. They already found it! And at an expensive price: LIFE.

This PANDEMIC shows that they do not sell to those who have the least; they wait for them to turn PURPLE, then they can pay the price.

For the rest of us, the AIR is rationed by confining us to the space of the house ... The announcement is clear: "DO NOT GO OUT or pay with your LIFE!".

DEATH has always been a reality, but they paint it more grotesque than it IS ... Now you have to die ALONE. No blessing, no family, no friends, no funeral. INCINE- RATED even if it was not your will.

I have convinced myself that the matter is SECRET ...

While Covid comes to me I am going to sleep, I hope it will not be forever ... (Fingers crossed).

Between Tale and Gossip

(April 29th)

Mr. Wind came to visit me

At first I thought "WELCOME", even though I closed doors and windows ... I said: "Give me the gift of rain, we need it!". I think he got mad because I didn't open the door. The alarms sounded ... The visitor was DANGEROUS!

I was scared! I no longer asked him for anything, what I wanted was for him to leave without hurting him. He whistled for a while and, to punish me, he stripped my trees of some branches, filled my yard with trash and rain. No drop ...! "I'm doing you GOOD, I'm destroying the old ...". I located myself in the PANDEMIC that we live and I raised a prayer to heaven: "LORD, do not leave me alone, give me the courage to overcome the fear of tomorrow."

Between Tale and Gossip

(April 29th)

Social distancing

I tell you ... In this collective SOLITUDE we have revalued what physical contact means.

When something is forbidden to us, it becomes our fervent desire to break the rule. This seems like an experiment: They bring us into a critical situation to measure our reactions. They are tightening the rope.

When I despair ... I go out to observe the garden. My flowers do HUG. The red lilies to his wonderful friends, and the white flower to a dry plant (his neighbor) that requires motivation.

My friends are so wise that they know how to do it with their time and on TIME.

WE WILL RETURN HUGS! Our time is yet to come.

Existence

I tell you, this unprecedented situation that we live leads me to reflect: "Either we coexist or we do not exist."

Man is a most adaptable being, he endures the most adverse circumstances and rises from his falls.

This photo is real, my classmates and I, teachers recently graduated from the Benemérita Normal de Coahuila, started work in Tierra Caliente (GRO). We found our ranches in a deplorable situation, they had suffered an earthquake that knocked down schools and left them more impoverished than before. Given this: We rebuild schools and organized we take the fallen.

I am sure that the teacher-student and student-teacher binomial is the unalterable formula of TEACHING.

It will be necessary to adapt to working with students who we do not see, who do not feel close, who do not raise their hands to ask ... but who continue to need us as much as we need them.

"Either we coexist ... or we don't exist." Better times will come.

Between Tale and Gossip

(April 25th)

Who is hiding?

I'll give enough clues for you to find it:

It is unspeakable, intangible, unbearable, inflexible, inhuman, indecipherable ...

Why do I tell you more if it is INVISIBLE. Ah! I forgot, he is UNDOCUMENTED, an illegal man who has crossed all borders without anyone being able to stop him. He has done a lot of damage, but he declares himself INNOCENT, he did not want to, they forced him ... WHO? ... They are also in hiding ...

Between Tale and Memory

(April 24th)

Let's think

Now that we have time ... who is to blame for this Hell? Today none of us are in Paradise.

We cannot point to guilty because the great culprit it is INVISIBLE.

It reminds me of a phrase from the great Aztec emperor, Cuauhtémoc ("falling eagle"): Am I on a bed of roses?

Our country, MEXICO, is in torment just like everybody. Let's not add fuel to the fire.

Between Tale and Gossip

(April 23rd)

Next to my rose is a small plant

I just bought the pots in the greenhouse; I had plenty $ 10.00, what could I buy with that coin?

I thought about telling the salesperson: "Keep the change." Ahead of my thoughts, he gave me this miniature and said: "This plant is called ABUNDANCE". To which I replied: "A small abundance, but ABUNDANCE at last."

Many of us have little abundance; others, a lot, and most, NOTHING.

But you know? GOD protects the underdog ...

Did you see the SEA giving away fish? In Acapulco IT HAPPENED.

BETWEEN TALE AND GOSSIP

(April, the 21st)

I tell you…

In my garden I observed these lilies very close together and half hidden … I stopped and, with a friendly tone, I said to them: "Friends, you are not keeping the SANE DISTANCE". I am aware that they did not listen to me, I laughed when I was speaking to myself (this is how this quarantine has me).

My lilies are not afraid to DIE, they know that their cycle ends when they wither.

We don't even understand withered skin.

What if this, what if the other, what if the rest … excess information … one step forward and one back.

But you know, it's not time to UNDERSTAND, it's time to OBEY.

(April 18th)

I saw this movie a long time ago and rediscovered the concepts it left me with.

One man's madness is said to be another man's children's book. The main character was an old ... eternal seeker of his home, he did not give up in his efforts to find that place; stated:

Something is worth dying for.
My home is the only place I have ever known. My kingdom is my only goal.
I love the word PEACE ... I come from there, I belong there. What is the point of being a KING without a kingdom.
I existed because I dreamed ... (just like me).

In the present I heard a president say: "What is the point of being a president without a people, it would be a dry leaf, a vase that has no other function than to decorate."

Between Tale and Gossip

(April 15th)

Love takes away fear

That couple did not use the mouth guard. What happiness!

When I saw her, I heard another couple say: "How beautiful it is to LOVE!"

"Yes," she said, "when you don't know what you're exposing yourself to, what you're risking."

His interlocutor replied: "They know what goes in the package; perhaps forgetfulness, deceit, heartbreak, difficulties, betrayal ... and yet they take risks. LIVING is a risk that we all take ".

I thought: "LOVE removes fear." And I remembered some verses:

Love is the right word that you need to face death.

Take my breath away, but not the POETRY!

Between Tale and Cinema

(April 13th)

Your Excellence

Good day to remember Cantinflas, excellent in His Excellency. In this film he expressed without chanting: "Half of humanity against the other half", Greens against Reds.

They never seem to understand what the humble carpenter from Nazareth came to teach us: "LOVE EACH OTHER", not "ARM each other".

The country of Los Cocos (I think it's us) does not know where to go.

He does not want the IDEOTas of the reds, nor the LOANS of the greens.

To make us all think alike is to make ROBOTS; Enslaving ourselves for money implies that we stop being FREE: Programmers and creditors, we do not want them knocking on our door, stripping ourselves of everything for not thinking alike or for even owing the air we breathe.

SO my vote is not for either of us.

I QUIT! I am a simple citizen, unimportant, without titles of nobility but FREE! ...

(I loved you, CANTINFLAS, sorry if I misspelled what you said so GOOD).

Between Tale and Memory

(April 7th)

Dialogue with President Amlo

Only old people can talk about old things ... Let's start:
"Sir, are you being criticized for speaking to shamans?"
"Yes, let them do it, I will continue to seek wisdom in my ancestors."
"Why do you wear charms and stamps?"
—It's not a sin, I have FAITH. Mexico is a believer and faithful.
—It seems that this is not normal for a president.
"If it's normal to be arrogant, corrupt and a liar, then I'm abnormal."
"Did you prepare the country for this crisis?"
"Since I started my mandate with programs for the forgotten."
"But ... is our health system neglected?"
"I'm picking up what my predecessors dropped."
"They say that the country with you is going to disaster."
—The worst pandemic is corruption, getting out of it will be painful, we are transforming ourselves.
- Will it rescue the economy of the big companies?
—Yes, but first the poor; I can't do another program until I see that what I planned is working out.
—The voices of the greats, you must also hear them ...
"I do, but minorities can wait."

—The majorities are being served.

"Is governing a secret office?"

—I don't hide anything every day I say what happens in the country. Transparency is my goal.

"Are you not afraid of the great interests that it has affected?"

"NO! People take care of me."

"Are you afraid of death?"

—She comes when she wants, I have no control over death.

I didn't want to ask any more because my president and that of all Mexicans is RIGHT.

NOTE: Sometimes being right is useless.

BETWEEN TALE AND GOSSIP

(April 4th)

What time do I teach?

This anecdote is relevant to what we are currently experiencing.

As a primary school teacher, the principal of my school called me and other teachers to the council meeting to notify us about the visit of the School Inspector.

"I want you to keep THIS in mind," he told us; on your desk, all your records and your activity planning. The children with their very clean hands and clipped nails. Well groomed, well behaved, no one outside the room… Oh, and they should put a mat on the door, not too wet, not too dry. The inspector is very strict and very demanding; I don't want attention calls, teachers. "

We all take note. A newcomer, a colleague, dared to ask: "If I have to do all this, what time do I teach?"

This is relevant because, waiting for COVID 19 with so many indications, protocols and rules, I feel like asking: "What time do I LIVE?

BETWEEN TALE AND GOSSIP

(April 1st)

Do you listen to the warnings?

Today my cell phone gave me the answer to this question: "The battery is running low", and I, close, close, close ... ignoring the warning not once, but several times.

What had to happen happened ... she turned black, HE DIED.

I had the vaccine and I did not apply it. I had a way of resuscitating her, but wow, I forgot the charger. I asked for one and you know, nobody wanted to lend it to me, they were busy to make their dying phones breathe.

I couldn't call anyone else, I was imprisoned in my house and my recklessness ... the cell phone seemed to yell at me: "I TOLD YOU! Careless, disbelieving, misinformed ...

I felt desperate, unmade, UNHAPPY. EVERYTHING FOR IGNORING THE NOTICES.

Between Tale and Legend

(March 29th)

Why does the donkey have big ears?

They say that one day the animals were lining up for the Creator to assign them a name. This is how the lion, the giraffe, the turtle passed by... Young and old were waiting their turn. When it was the donkey's turn, they said: "You will be called ...

DONKEY!". "He's fine," he said, "but he had barely walked a few steps before he forgot. He returned and asked again: "What is my name?" THE LORD thought: "I think I made a mistake with your ears, I'll make them a little bigger", and he did ... but the donkey forgot several times and although all his animal companions were shouting: "Donkey! Donkey! "He did not understand and the Lord, with the patience of a saint, continued to enlarge his ears.

The most cruel punishment that I witnessed as a child was having a classmate sent to the corner, with donkey ears.

MORAL: We walk many burritos around the world that we do not understand STAY AT HOME. And you know what? The punishment will be cruel, sent not by a teacher, but by Mrs. DEATH who is on the loose ... Our GOD can no longer make our ears bigger to see if we understand, he is very busy balancing the BOAT where we are ALL going .

Between Tale and Gossip

(March 28th)

Let's not spread fear

Today I dedicated myself to sanitizing which, as I understand it, is to clean and disinfect all the spaces in my house. I took special care of my body, my hands. Now that I'm alone and doing the dishes, my hands are super clean. I do not use the sanitizing gel because they peel and burn. I am grateful to God that he has brought me back to chores: I can already distinguish salt from sugar. I have time to watch the news; Wrong! Because it makes me want to complain, blame, criticize and, then, the cleanliness of the outside does not check with my inner state. Sanitizing is not the same as SATANIZING. My crazy mind takes me where I don't want to. Being afraid is not an option, we would end up in panic. If sane we do not give one, uncontrolled less!

Let's clean our insides, let's not let the enemy in. To the perverse mind that leads you to the negative, say: "OUT! OUTSIDE!". Don't let fear lead you to Hell.

(March 27th)

Thank you Holy Pope

Today in a lonely square, converted into a temple next to Christ, in pain and bleeding, our POPE, the one chosen to guide the flock, spoke to us about not being afraid in the storm because CHRIST is awake and will go to straighten the boat where we are going everybody...

I felt PEACE emanating from his white garment, his sweet expression and his fatigue.

I cried my guilt, I was filled with the Holy Spirit, I received his BLESSING and I sang: "GOD is here ... as true as the air I breathe ... GOD IS HERE!".

Between Tale and Gossip

(March 19th)

Friends, read me!

The restraining measures of the eastern countries must be followed:

RESTRAIN to leave. RESTRAIN to travel. RESTRAIN to disobey. RESTRAIN to be irresponsible. RESTRAIN to endanger your health and that of others.
RESTRAIN even to show love.
With so much advertising of everything I CONTINUE.

In the Mexican philosophy, according to Octavio Paz, "The other dies", not me, or at least not yet ... The only condition to DIE is to be ALIVE and you and I are.
RESTRAIN to DIE.
I know that at the end of this pause, from holding back so much, we will restart ... If we manage to get out of the RESTRAINING pandemic, in peace and grateful to GOD, it will have been worth fighting the battle ...

Between Tale and Poetry

(April 14th)

The magic

When I was a child I used to listen to songs and radio soap operas at my grandmother's house. When she went out to the patio, I stared at the device, it had magic! And I wanted to see it. I thought that if I opened the back cover I would find the singers and the characters kissing.

But NO! What a disappointment ... there were only bulbs and wires. Magic became possible when television arrived, although it was lost when the power went out.

Later, the MAGIC was even greater when the computer arrived and YOU KNOW, now I don't see novels; those behind (I don't know) look at MY NOVEL.

They even know how I sleep, what I eat, who I hang out with and the most dangerous, even how I THINK.

My fingerprints are on the computer and I have not been able to discover the trick.

What I am sure of is that I want to remain flesh and blood, not a SHADOW trapped in a CHIP.

Between Tale and Poetry

(April 10th)

What did the poets say in the midst of other crises?

Progress has uninhabited man, we have more things but no more BEING.

OCTAVIO PAZ

No one will have the right to superfluity, / while someone lack the strict.

SALVADOR DÍAZ MIRÓN

A man dies in me / whenever a man / is murdered / by the hatred and bullets of other men.

JAIME TORRES BODET

What if it hurts? A little ... / I confess that you treacherously hurt me / more fortunately after the rage / came a sweet resignation.

LUIS G. URBINA

Let your own effort / be like a powerful microscope / that is finding invisible universes / and then in the flame of the bonfire / of an infinite and superhuman love / As the saint of Assisi you will say brother / to the tree to the clouds and to the beast.

ENRIQUE GONZÁLEZ MARTÍNEZ

All, Mexican poets, inviting us to return to BEING human buried in materialism and unreason.

BETWEEN TALE AND MEMORY

(April 9th)

Holy Thursday

Listening today to the Mass given from the Basilica of Saint Peter in the Vatican, my eyes stopped on the HOLY SPIRIT, our great COMFORTER.
These words from the Homily of the
HOLY FATHER: "Service is LOVE."
Our clumsiness is so great that the world had to stop so that we would stop talking and learn to LISTEN ...
From the silence we receive the PEACE of the LORD; Our great comforter tells us: "We will return HUGS", because the blood of the lamb is a drink that purifies us ...
Amen...

Between Tale and Gossip

(April 8th)

What does the strong say to the weak?

Only "No! No! No!".

Don't move, don't go out, don't vacation, don't talk, no shake hands, don't hug, don't medicate, no, no, no. We are playing statues and charmed.

Faced with such adverse circumstances, an old man asked me: "Do you understand?"; "Well, I understand that it is for our good"; "No, teacher, I understand that they want us to disappear, they just need to order us to STOP BREATHING. Old cans in the trash ".

I thought about my years and reasoned the same. I did not want to take away the HOPE to continue living and I told him: "Don't hurry, they will DISENCHANT us."

Between Tale and Memory

(April 6th)

We are on our knees

For the first time what happens to us has brought the world to its knees ... imploring SALVATION.

Our daily prayer is inclusive. We ask for our children, our family, our people, our country and the whole world.

For the first time we recognize that the other is important, that we all need EVERYONE:

The uncertainty of dying has united us. Mrs. DEATH, the most democratic ... the one who equals us all in her dark enclosure, today she does it on earth, in the sunlight. If we know how to listen, we will hear her say: "Why do you want to escape from me? To continue HATING".

Friends, may our prayer be to return to embrace and LOVE.

Tale And Film

Autumn days

This movie from the 60s, shot in black and white, won several awards. I will summarize the plot: The protagonist of the film, dressed as a bride, stands in the atrium of the church. She was never able to assimilate the trauma this caused her. She worked in a pastry shop, the boss was in love with her, but he knew she was married. It seemed strange not knowing her husband. One day he asked her: "Why does he never come for you?" "He travels a lot," she said. He took her home. "You don't have a wedding photo ...". She had it done. Time passed and the boss kept observing: "Why haven't you gotten pregnant?" She faked a pregnancy, she lived alone and at night she read these verses: "If we can't love / and the night moves on / let's make an alliance / With that fake dream / Oblivion will come / or HOPE will end". In her, oblivion did not come, but hope did end: she committed SUICIDED!

I pray that this does not happen to us, that we save hope that give LOVE.

Story And Film

On racism and xenophobia

In this blessed break in which I find myself, in the evening I saw the movie Hidden Talents, which is about the NASA space race. Something very redeemable in this film is the story of three women of color who, with their struggle and their knowledge, managed to work in this space agency, despite being discriminated against and despised.

They faced the challenge and conquered it ... America owes them a lot. When the heroine, who appears in the photo, was reprimanded for taking 40 minutes to return from the bathroom, because the bathrooms intended for black ladies were far from the office, something happened ... The boss absorbed the lesson, removed the letters-reserved bathtubs and said, "Here at NASA, everyone we urinate the same color ".

Women were not allowed into high-level meetings, least of all a woman of color, but she knew answers that others did not. And it happened.

The director told the deputy bosses: "Our job is to observe the best and find the genius within them. If that genius wins, we all win; if we don't find out, we all lose ".

America owes a lot to non-white brains and the brains of immigrants. Progress is a double-edged sword ... It takes us to the moon, but it makes us lose our ground.

Let's stop our wars ... Stop HATING. The women in this film were not invented; are real.

Story And Film

(April 5th)

Splendor in the grass

I'm going back to my past to get out of it, YOUTH, as the song says.

I remember seeing a movie, Splendor in the grass, which gave my students an example so that their love stories would not go through traumatic situations.

It is the story of impossible love, not realized even when the couple was united by that wonderful feeling.

What I remember most are some verses that the star of the film read in her classroom.

"Though the day / of splendor on the grass will never return ... / Nor the glory of the flower, we will find / STRENGTH in what remains ".

We have all lost a lot along the way, we face adversity and pain, but you know? We will find STRENGTH in what we have left. My strength is GOD that everything that is not seen, but FEELS.

Between Art, Story and Myth

(April 2nd)

What is Metamorphosis?

At school they told me: It is changing from one stage to another without looking like the previous one, for example, the cocoon does not look like the caterpillar, nor the caterpillar like the butterfly ... They have a family resemblance, but they changed.

How beautiful are the BUTTERFLIES! Could it be for this reason that at the end of the plague box that Pandora came to spread, God left a little green butterfly that, by flying in that plagued world, gave HOPE back to man?

Yesterday I chased a white butterfly that perched on my flowers gave me PEACE.

One of ANNE GEDDES's paintings, which I have in my house, shows how wings are being born to this humanity. We are TRANSFORMING.

Between Tale and Legend

(March 30th)

Why do bats have wings?

According to CATÓN, my favorite writer from Coahuila, when a child asked his mother this, she replied: "They have wings so that the mice think there are angels." The child grew up and now he knows or thinks he knows that bats are angels, but angels of DEATH !, and SATANIZED them ...

The good news is that bats don't know. But men are AFRAID.

Between poetry, art and roads

My Pray

(April 29th)

Before defeated columns I ask your favor, my GOD ... Before the pace that is already slow give me wings to fly.

In the face of tired life give me the strength of the sea ... In the black of sorrow, come to ease my pain.

May this unpolished mirror reflect your LOVE.

Dreaming...

(April 22nd)

I am dreaming that I dream of making another existence, of transparent windows that project new light.

Eyes that penetrate the various horizons that seek, with their gaze, to explain this mystery hidden in valleys and mountains ...

A voice made a bell that calls everyone to mass,
to love each other without conditions, to love each other leaving the soul.

Hands with the softness of a dove that, when touching, leave tenderness, transform our clay
and erase all bitterness ...

A selective heart that houses only the good,
pick flowers and trills, and beautify the trail.

Walking new paths to meet my beloved with a light dress and an ethereal wedding veil, walking on the sea, seeking to touch the ... HEAVEN!

Thank You Doctors

(April 22nd)

When pain touches your life
there is a doctor who will heal the wound.

When health is broken there is a doctor who restores HOPE ...

When the miracle of BORN is announced,
a doctor takes him in his hands and hugs him.

When the cycle is closed and DEATH arrives with her cruel sword ...
it is a doctor who gives
the news and testifies to the end of human existence.

Let's not forget to THANK that army in the white coat, their beautiful profession ... the one that SAVES because it LOVES !!!

Signals

(April 17th)

Everything languishes with the years. Hope does not die ... sheltered by the last dreams it refuses to abandon us.

FLOWERS FOR THE VIRGIN

(April 17th)

Spring in my house, spring in my soul asking you, my mother, HOPE ... FAITH ... VALUE. Intercede with the FATHER for this contrite world that forgot LOVE ...

Spring Arrived

(March 21st)

It is March 21, spring is announced.
The grass is dressed in green, roses and lilies bloom. I hear the sparrows sing.

The LORD waters my trees,
its deep roots require water from heaven. Like us who, in our aridity,
We look up for an answer to our prayers.

Spring makes the earth and our HOPE reborn.

My Visitors

(April 18th)

These precious birds are also with me in the campaign ... STAY HOME, I almost heard them trilling ... when this happens, they will surely FLY!

I Long

(April 18th)

I long for the sun
my patio smelling of honeysuckle ...

The night comes, erase my tracks ...

We spend like everyone casting a shadow and from time to time we LOVE and LOVE us.

My Home

(April 17th)

This I do in MY HOUSE
in quarantine days:

The world stays outside, The world lives inside, A world that those of us at home Imagine PERFECT.

* *

My house tastes like HARMONY, my house smells HAPPY, my house has that something
of OASIS in a desert.

OLDER BROTHER

Resurrected Christ,
JESUS of the mercy of forgiveness and love, you walk all the roads,
my broken Christ, my lonely Christ, I shelter myself in your heart ...

The Undesirable

(April 11th)

She, the great liberator, watches from afar
and knowing undesirable slows the pace,
but it's on the prowl.

Keep playing with your dice, hiding the scythe,
without stopping our clock passes by.

She gives time to time, she knows when
her stealth march
it will send us calm, it will lead us to silence.

We will float in a new space of unsuspected light;
We will be complete PEACE leaving matter to inhabit the SOUL.

Holy Friday

(April 11th)

The sadness of GOOD FRIDAY has penetrated deep. Even those who call themselves atheists must be moved by the pain of the Lamb, our savior. Slain to save us. He washed away our sins with his blood, and humanity continues to sin. Today the glory opens so that we understand the great LOVE of the son of God.

We await his resurrection because his promise to give us ETERNAL LIFE is fulfilled. We have FAITH. Christ lives!

New Day

(April 11th)

Tomorrow ... maybe tomorrow I'll find what I'm looking for; yesterday I searched without finding, Tomorrow ... maybe tomorrow.

Future, I can't tell you apart
Did you arrive without being noticed?

My dreams need you, don't forget me, I beg you! Dressed for spring, I'm ready to receive you
Will you go to the appointment?
The new time smiles leaving me a promise! TOMORROW ... maybe tomorrow.

My Shadow

(April 2nd)

My shadow leaves no room for emptiness ...
Permanent guest,
fills my body like ivy, imprisons me, chases me in the sun, in the rain.
At night it seems,
that escapes ... it frees me ... but No !, it embraces me all.

I'm scared! She ... LAUGHS.

FRIEND

(April 1st)

I'm walking
in the small space of my confinement.
So long! And I do not arrive at the port of your embrace.
To look at you
I have opened my window. I looked for you in the wind, I got lost
in your SEA.

Adam and Eve

(March 30th)

Adam, if you were the only man on Earth, maybe I would look at you, maybe holding your hand I would win my war ...
Without having to doubt, without having to suffer; neither laugh nor cry ...

All synthesized in you, only in YOU. At the voice of YA !, I would choose you.
Very sure of myself I clicked ... A VIRUS was introduced,
the moon went out
in my dark night, my dream ended ...

I am ALONE.

Lucid discoveries

(July 19th)

I DISCOVERED THAT:
Old age is not contagious. It is accumulated health.
"The worst thing about getting old is not getting there."

(July 18th)

I DISCOVERED THAT:
Traffic lights
they last forever ... all on
Confusing us!
COVID-19 does not want to give us the green light ...

(July 11th)

I DISCOVERED THAT:
If COVID-19 still has so much rating
they are going to add CHAPTERS.

(July 5th)

I DISCOVERED THAT:
We are hostages of the invisible.
We will continue dancing to the SON that touches us.

I DISCOVERED THAT:
We are hiding playing "You bring it and you don't hit it".
We are all SUSPICIOUS.

(June 25th)

I DISCOVERED THAT:
I don't want to be an old thing
forgotten in a cellar.
Best "LISTED ANTIQUITY".

(June 22nd)

I DISCOVERED THAT:
The hugs are still FROZEN.
Now I understand
because social relationships get cold.

(June 21st)

I DISCOVERED THAT:
My new occupation is that of
lighthouse described in the story
The Little Prince ...
I have the task of turning off the lantern in the
morning and turning it on at night. I feel useful!

(June 18th)

I DISCOVERED THAT:
The fountain of eternal youth does exist ...
but not for the body but for the SPIRIT.

(May 19th)

I DISCOVERED THAT:
A day of LIGHT
worth a lot of DARK.

I DISCOVERED THAT:
The HEART of the sower remains in his CREATION.
In this forced pause we have returned to ESSENCE.

Nature has a lot to tell us when we connect with the
CREATOR.

(May 17th)

I DISCOVERED THAT: :
I'm GUESS
but only what is in front of my eyes.

(May 16th)

I DISCOVERED THAT:
I ask God for energy, strength ... he barely gives me
and ABUSE ...

I DISCOVERED THAT:
OLD flip flops
they are comfortable,
but they cause serious stumbling.

I DISCOVERED THAT:
The DOUBT eats me:
Do they incinerate the dead of COVID
so ... that there is no trace, what not and what not,
that there is no FOOTPRINT ... ",
sorry, I'm listening to BRONCO ...

(May 15th)

I DISCOVERED THAT:
The SMALL details make the BIG effects ...

(May 14th)

I DISCOVERED THAT:
The old and the new COEXIST ...
but we are a GENERATION that says GOODBYE.

(May 13th)

I DISCOVERED THAT:
HUGS are in portfolio EXPIRED ...
I owe a lot and I can't pay.

(May 12th)

I DISCOVERED THAT:
A vulgar THIEF
and another of WHITE NECK participate in the same crime:
the first, PUNISHED;
the second, FREE due to lack of evidence.

(May 11th)

I DISCOVERED THAT: :
It is important to SAY, but even more so, TO DO!

(May 10th)

I DISCOVERED THAT:
The mothers
they are people specialized in the IMPOSSIBLE.

(May 9th)

I DISCOVERED THAT:
This quarantine has caused
that the smile is not seen on the lips, but in the eyes.

(May 8th)

I DISCOVERED THAT:
The mask is ANTI AGE,
covers wrinkles, scars, toothpaste and helps social outreach.

(May 7th)

I DISCOVERED THAT:
If in a shipwreck you lose EVERYTHING,
but YOU are saved,
you have not lost ANYTHING.

(May 6th)

I DISCOVERED THAT:
I would like to bottle the TIME
to drink one by one my memories ...

I DISCOVERED THAT:
There is always SOMETHING that stays with us,
of so much and so much that we are leaving ...

(May 5th)

I DISCOVERED THAT:
2020 is a twin year, "we are giving birth twins" ...

(May 4th)

I DISCOVERED THAT:
When we are open to criticism we have a COUNCIL.

(May 3rd)

I DISCOVERED THAT:
This year he has not let us LIVE IT; stole half of us.
I DISCOVERED THAT: T
he day will come to be ONE with the EARTH.

(May 2nd)

I DISCOVERED THAT:
If the OTHER appropriates me, I am no longer.

I DISCOVERED THAT:
When I pay attention to the OTHER
I am giving a valuable gift ... my TIME.

(May 1st)

I DISCOVERED THAT:
Opening and closing your eyes is not automatic.
You also LEARN.
Some of us learn it fast; others, NEVER.

(April 29th)

I DISCOVERED THAT:
The birds look for the dry branches to give them their song
and brighten up your moments,
before falling down in the wind.

I DISCOVERED THAT:
I'm not the girl who plays with you
I am a double mom, a crazy GRANDMA.

I DISCOVERED THAT:
I am alone in the silence that the soul asks to continue
LIVING.

I DISCOVERED THAT:
Memories
they are GOLD dust attached to TODAY.

(April 28th)

I DISCOVERED THAT:
Love out of pity, hurts.

(April 27th)

I DISCOVERED THAT:
In the social distancing we live in,
not even the shadow embraces us.

I DISCOVERED THAT:
Seeing without hugging is a TORTURE.

(April 26th)

I DISCOVERED THAT:
Seeing the SUN HOPE is renewed.

(April 25th)

I DISCOVERED THAT:
Ignoring biased information is HEALTHY.
Will you know how to distinguish it?

(April 24th)

I DISCOVERED THAT:
When the other is HELL
you are not PARADISE.

I DISCOVERED THAT:
You have to reread the Diary of Anne Frank to understand CONFINEMENT. History repeats itself.

(April 22nd)

I DISCOVERED THAT:
COVID does not enter the covered mouth.

I DISCOVERED THAT:
I haven't said for a long time
"Time flew by," and what I do every day
I already do it "With my eyes closed."

(April 20th)

I DISCOVERED THAT:
Being on the trip is the important thing.
The movement has stopped
the day passes from bright to cloudy;
here I am anchored in the present ...
Because the FUTURE does not let me reach it.

I DISCOVERED THAT:
The wind left me a beautiful gift.
I THANK YOU, I will not sweep today.

(April 19th)

I DISCOVERED THAT:
Believing without Seeing is true FAITH.

(April 18th)

I DISCOVERED THAT:
The first smile of this day was for ME
and ENCOURAGED me.

(April 17th)

I DISCOVERED THAT:
"Your house can replace the world but not everyone
can replace your HOUSE"

(April 16th)

I DISCOVERED THAT:
Weaving and unweaving my moments I find that
I have advanced in weaving.

I DISCOVERED THAT:
The Sun as a witness
confirm with the wind
the adventure of the day that we have to LIVE.

(April 15th)

I DISCOVERED THAT:
Love on the skin
It is an explosion of auroras.

(April 14th)

I DISCOVERED THAT:
We old people need LITTLE,
but that little, we need it a LOT.

(April 13th)

I DISCOVERED THAT:
The OLD are like the SUN
that at sunset gives us its most beautiful radiance.

(April 12th)

He had to stop the world to stop
TALKING and learn to LISTEN.

Contents

Instants

Between Tale And...

Quarantine Effects	17
Death has permission ...	18
The snow ball	19
Do they sell us air?	20
Mr. Wind came to visit me	21
Social distancing	23
Existence	24
Who is hiding?	26
Let's think	27
Next to my rose is a small plant	28
I tell you...	29
Love takes away fear	31
Your Excellence	32
Dialogue with President Amlo	33
What time do I teach?	35
Do you listen to the warnings?	36
Why does the donkey have big ears?	37
Let's not spread fear	39
Thank you Holy Pope	40
Friends, read me!	41
The magic	42
What did the poets say in the midst of other crises?	43
Holy Thursday	45
What does the strong say to the weak?	46

We are on our knees 47
Autumn days 48
On racism and xenophobia 49
Splendor in the grass 50
What is Metamorphosis? 51
Why do bats have wings? 52

Between poetry, art and roads

My Pray 55
Dreaming 56
Thank You Doctors 58
Signals 59
Flowers For The Virgin 60
Spring Arrived 62
My Visitors 63
I Long 64
My Home 65
Older Brother 67
The Undesirable 68
Holy Friday 69
New Day 70
My Shadow 71
Friend 73
Adam and Eve 74

Lucid discoveries